DIGORY
THE DRAGON SLAYER

ANGELA MCALLISTER
illustrated by Ian Beck

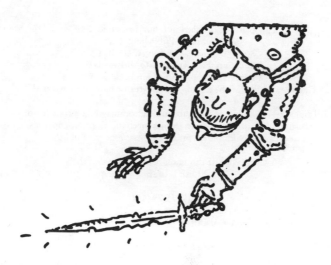

BLOOMSBURY

This edition published in Great Britain in 2005
by Bloomsbury Publishing Plc,
36 Soho Square, London, W1D 3QY
Text copyright © Angela McAllister 2005
Illustrations copyright © Ian Beck 2005
The moral rights of the author and illustrator have been asserted

A CIP record of this book is available from the
British Library

ISBN 0 7475 7944 X

Printed in Great Britain by Clays Ltd, St Ives plc

10 9 8 7 6 5 4 3 2 1

All papers used by Bloomsbury Publishing are natural, recyclable products
made from wood grown in well-managed forests.
The manufacturing processes conform to the environmental
regulations of the country of origin.

For Sam — A.M.
For Lily — I.B.

CONTENTS

Chapter One

In Days of Old

IN days of old, when knights were bold, there lived a boy called Digory. He came from a village where nothing much happened and he was just a bit older than you.

Digory had lanky legs, ginger hair and a nose like a chipolata. This made him very popular with the village boys.

'Skittle legs!' they called him.

'Stick boy!'

'Oi, pumpkin head!'

'Hey, marigold bonce!'

'Digory droopy-dangle!'

'Nose jouster!'

'Sausage snout!'

Digory wore a felt cap to hide his ginger hair but he couldn't disguise that nose, so he kept away from the village and spent his days playing alone in the forest.

Digory loved the forest. Some days he'd build dams and tree houses. Some days he'd poke about with sticks and think thoughts. You might think he was lonely but he had one friend who followed him everywhere – a battered old lute from his father that he carried across his back. When Digory thought some interesting thoughts he'd turn them into a song, climb a tree and sing to the sparrows.

Now, none of his family understood Digory at all. His older brothers, Arthur and Tom, were big and tough and bold. Arthur won prizes for hog leaping and Tom was the local turnip tossing champion. The thoughts they had were mostly to do with chasing bulls and arm wrestling, and the songs they knew were drinking songs, which had to be shouted wildly as you poured a flagon of beer over your head.

The only time Arthur called for Digory was to keep watch when he was stealing apples, and the only time Tom needed Digory was to pick up the arrows after archery practice.

Even his sister Ethelburg, captain of the Mucky Maidens' Mudflinging team, had no time for Digory.

'Ear shriveller!' she would cry whenever he played the lute, and put a basket over her head.

When he wasn't in the forest, Digory would hang around the forge where his mother Betsy the blacksmith worked, hoping she might notice him. But nobody heard Digory strumming and singing except his father.

'You know your mother, son,' he said gently as he pegged out the washing. 'She likes iron and fire and sweat and muscles. She doesn't have much time for thinking and songs.'

'Unless they're songs about iron and fire and sweat and muscles!' shouted his mother from the smithy, as she pounded her hammer on the anvil.

But Digory's songs weren't like that. They had lines that went:

> *'See the happy swans that float,*
> *Round the castle's rippling moat.*
> *Hear the water lilies sigh,*
> *As the dragonflies dart by.'*

Well, nobody wanted to listen to that. So Digory's family left him to wander with the forest animals, playing songs to himself, poking about in streams and thinking thoughts.

13

Digory never got into much trouble in the forest. Sometimes an acorn fell on his head. Sometimes he stepped into a pile of wild pig poo. But one day he found something that caused a little misunderstanding. Something that changed his life for ever. Something that made him wish with all his heart that he'd stepped in a pile of pig poo instead.

Digory had spent all morning making a stick bridge over a stream. Pleased with himself, he sat down and started to unpack his picnic. But, just as he bit into a dandelion pasty, he noticed a white thing glinting on the mossy bank. Digory peered closer. It was a large, sharp, jagged tooth.

Who does this belong to? he wondered, picking it up. *Maybe it's a rabbit's tooth?* But it was far too big for a rabbit. *Then perhaps it's a witch's tooth*, he thought, *and maybe she'll come looking to use it in a spell!* But he remembered that witches always have rotten teeth and this one was white and sharp.

Suddenly a creepy feeling made his hair stand on end. *Suppose it's a giant's tooth*, he trembled. *And suppose the giant isn't very far away . . . SUPPOSE I'M SITTING ON THE TOE OF HIS GREEN LEATHER BOOT AT THIS VERY MINUTE!*

Digory didn't dare look behind him. But he trembled so much that he pricked himself on the tooth. Wrapping a handkerchief round his finger he began to laugh. *Daft dunderhead!* he chuckled. *This is much too pointy for a giant's tooth. It must have belonged to an animal . . . a large animal . . . a large, fierce animal . . . something as large and fierce as a DRAGON!!*

Digory decided that was his best thought. *Yes, it's definitely a dragon's tooth*, and he stuck it into his hat. Then, after all that difficult thinking, he scoffed a large piece of honeycomb cake and a bag of bramble jellybeans.

When the picnic was finished Digory made up a song called 'The Truth of the Tooth'!

This was definitely *not* one of Digory's greatest songs, but the words fitted a tune that had been humming itself in his head for days, so he was very pleased.

Later that afternoon, as he wandered along the lane, Digory met Noggy Bowlegs, the goose boy, leading his geese to market.

'Don't reckon the tooth fairy will notice that molar up there on your hat,' Noggy giggled. 'Better put it under your pillow when you get home.'

'That's not my tooth,' said Digory, giving Noggy a grin to show that he had none missing. 'That's a dragon's tooth!'

At the mention of the word 'dragon' Noggy's knees began to quiver.

'Oooh! Oddsbodikins!' he gasped. 'Now don't you say another word there, Digory,' he stuttered. 'You'll scare the geese so much they'll be as thin as old boilers by the time I get them to market.'

Poor Noggy looked so awestruck that Digory couldn't help himself.

'DRRRAAAGGGONS!' he cried, waving his arms wildly. And, before you could say 'goosey, goosey, gander', Noggy and his birds had flown off down the lane.

NEWS TRAVELS FAST

Now, when Digory got home that afternoon, all the villagers stared. They pointed at his hat, nudging and whispering. At first, Digory, humming the tooth song to himself, didn't notice. Then someone started to cheer. People came running from the market and began to clap and whistle. Digory started to feel uncomfortable. He looked round. No, there wasn't an Important Person riding behind him. Even the village boys were cheering Digory himself.

Soon crowds had come out of their shops and cottages to get a glimpse of Digory passing by.

'Three cheers for Digory!' they cried.

'Digory killed the dragon!'

17

The children jumped up to touch his hat.

'Look at the tooth, just like Noggy said! Digory has saved us from the dragon! Hurray, we're saved!'

Digory suddenly understood.

'But . . . but . . .' he protested. 'You've got it all wrong. I just found the tooth, I didn't even *see* a dragon.'

However, it was useless to argue. No one would listen. Digory found himself lifted on to the shoulders of the crowd and carried like a hero into the square, where the whole village had gathered and Squire Paunch himself was waiting.

Digory had always been shy of Squire Paunch. The Squire wore yellow waistcoats and black whiskers and slapped people on the back to be friendly. Digory wanted to run away, but there was nowhere to hide. The Squire brought his big whiskery face close to Digory's nose and peered at him with a puzzled look.

'Is this *him*?' he asked the crowd.

All the villagers cheered.

'YES!' they cried. 'That's him!'

So the Squire shook Digory by the hand and, sure enough, slapped him heartily on the back, (denting the lute and knocking all the breath out of him).

'Well, well,' the Squire laughed, 'who'd have thought that young carrot top here would single-handedly save our village from the dragon!'

'The bloodthirsty dragon!' cried a plough-boy in the crowd.

'The bone-crunching, snout-snarling, bloodthirsty dragon!' bellowed the butcher.

'The jaw-dripping, flesh-ripping, bone-crunching, snout-snarling, bloodthirsty dragon!' cackled an old dame at the back.

The villagers roared.

But all this flesh-ripping talk made Digory feel dizzy.

'Speech, speech!' shouted the crowd.

The Squire pushed Digory forward. All the villagers hushed to hear his words. Digory stared at their eager faces.

'I think . . . I think . . . I . . . eeuuurgh . . .'

And he swayed and he swooned and he faint-ed on the spot.

At that moment Digory's mother arrived. She pushed her way through the crowd with a hot poker.

'Make way, make way! Where's my boy? Where's my little Digory?' And, with a sweep of her strong arms, she picked Digory up off the ground, shook the dust off him and heaved him over her shoulder. The crowd cheered again.

'You should be very proud of your son, Betsy,' said the Squire. 'He's a great hero. He has saved this village from the jaw-dripping, flesh-ripping, bone-crunching, snout-snarling, bloodthirsty dragon. We'll have a feast in his honour. Why, we'll make him a knight and name him 'Sir Digory the Dragon Slayer'!'

Digory's mother beamed brighter than a furnace, and a hot tear sizzled down her face.

'That's my boy,' she sniffed proudly. 'I did-n't know he had it in him.' Then, curtseying to the Squire in her leather apron, she carried Digory off home to dunk him in the water barrel.

A FEW WORDS ABOUT CLEVERNESS

Now, the name of Digory's village was Batty-by-Noodle, which may give you some idea of the sort of people who lived there. No one from Batty had ever done anything clever.

One night Farmer Ragwort saw a shooting star fall into the pond but, though he fished all night, he never caught it. And Meg the cowgirl claimed she could talk to cows, but nobody was interested to hear what a cow had to say, so they didn't think much of that.

People thought Squire Paunch was the cleverest man in the village because he was the Squire. But none of them was clever enough to know *how* clever he really was. And the Squire himself, if he *was* clever, didn't know anyone cleverer to compare himself to, so how could he tell? Well, you get the picture.

So, when Digory came home with a dragon's tooth in his hat no one thought too hard about it. Somehow it slipped their minds that Batty-by-Noodle never had dragons living nearby. In fact, it was quite the wrong sort of a place for dragons altogether. There were no rocky caves, the forest was thin and weedy and most days it drizzled with rain, which of course is not healthy for a dragon's fiery breath. Who's going to be afraid of a dragon that only snorts steam from its nostrils?

But, you see, you would need to be clever to know this sort of thing.

So when the Batty villagers saw a tooth and heard it came from a dragon they believed without doubt that they'd all been spared a horrible fate.

THE UNHAPPY DAY

Meanwhile, a feast was arranged, with a ceremony to make Digory a knight, and nothing Digory could say would persuade anybody otherwise. If he tried to explain the truth people just thought he was being modest, which made him even more of a hero.

Arthur and Tom were very jealous that their younger brother had fought with a dragon. They tried to make Digory tell them about it by twisting his arm in twelve painful ways. But, as there was nothing to tell, Digory didn't say a word. At last they gave up and shook his poor numb hand in admiration.

'You're a good chap, brother Digory,' they said.

'Nobody likes a person who boasts about what he's done. You deserve to be a knight. We're proud of you.'

And so he even won the respect of his bold, tough brothers.

But poor Digory didn't want to be a knight. In fact, he didn't even know what knights were expected to do.

He asked his father, who was collecting eggs

in the garden. His father sat down and scratched his head.

'Well now, Digory,' he puzzled, 'I could tell you what the baker does, or the miller, but I've never met a knight, son. They say knights are always chivalrous, but I don't know what chivalrous is.'

'It sounds like the sort of thing you feel when you have coughs and sneezes,' said Digory glumly. His father agreed.

(Poor Digory. He might have felt better if he'd known that chivalrous *really* meant kind, honourable and brave. Still, that wasn't the worst of it . . .)

'Well then,' continued his father, 'when they're feeling all chivalrous they ride around the land saving damsels in distress.'

Digory's heart sank. The only damsel he knew was Ethelburg, and she was certainly never in distress. In fact, some people might say that Ethelburg and her friends *caused* quite a bit of distress around the village with their mudflinging and wild rampaging games. Digory always tried to keep well away when the distress was happening.

'Oh yes,' his father remembered, 'and you probably have to marry a princess too. That won't be so bad, son, will it?'

Ugh! A princess! Digory felt even more miserable. He tried to imagine Ethelburg cleaned up a bit, with a crown on her head, but this only made him feel worse. With a heavy heart he went off to the woods.

As he shuffled through the leaves Digory thought about what had happened. *How did everything get into such a muddle?* he sighed. *I was having such a simple sort of life, a* Digory *sort of life, with songs and trees and picnics in it. Now I have to go away and be a knight, feeling* shiverous *and looking for distress. If only I hadn't picked up that tooth in the forest.* And, climbing up into an acorn tree, he composed a sad song called 'The Unhappy Day'.

Meanwhile, Digory's mother hammered away to make him a suit of armour out of some snips and scraps that were lying around in the smithy. The armour was quite a good fit, although it squeaked and had a bit of a handle on the back that looked suspiciously like part of a watering can. But her *pièce de resistance* was the helmet, on top of which she had welded the dragon's tooth!

When Digory put the armour on it felt cold and clammy inside. *Maybe this is what* shiverous *means,* he thought gloomily. But his mother was so proud she actually gave him a hug. (Although Digory, of course, couldn't feel the hug inside his tin suit.)

'Oh, it fits like a gauntlet, son!' she sighed happily. 'I suppose I could have built a couple of extra inches into the tin boots but, never mind, no one will notice when you are sitting on your horse.'

All knights, of course, must have a horse for their adventures, and Squire Paunch kindly gave Digory a trusty steed. Barley the carthorse knew as much about adventures as Digory did about being a knight. She was old and gentle but she was deaf as a pumpkin. (*Well, at least she won't have to listen to Digory's songs,* Betsy thought to herself.)

 ## ARISE, SIR DIGORY?

The big day arrived. Digory woke up and pinched himself, but it was all real. He looked at Arthur and Tom snoring away like happy warthogs. *Maybe I'll just slip away,* he thought. *No one would really miss me. They could make Arthur a knight instead. He'd be much better at shiveriness than me . . .*

Digory didn't have to think too long to decide that running away was, in fact, a very good idea. Quiet as a mouse, he wrote a note to Squire Paunch, explaining that he wanted his brother Arthur to be the knight instead. Then he packed everything he owned into his best handkerchief and tied it to the end of a stick.

Whispering goodbye to his sleeping father, he crept quietly out of the cottage to make his escape. But at the door he met Betsy, who had been up all night polishing the armour.

'Spit and elbow grease, nothing to beat it!' she beamed. 'Today's the best day of my life, son. You've made me as proud as a big, brass bell!'

Poor Digory smiled weakly. You can't run away from that, can you?

Squire Paunch had announced that day was to be a holiday, so the village was decked with flags and flowers and the inn served free ale and hog-roast.

At midday, a procession arrived at Digory's cottage. With a ring on her anvil Betsy sent Digory off, squeaking gently on toothless old Barley, to be knighted by Squire Paunch.

In the square, the rest of the villagers had been waiting impatiently. Everyone cheered loudly when Digory arrived, but the Squire himself did not appear. They waited and waited. Digory shut his eyes and wished with all his heart that the Squire had changed his mind and gone fishing instead. However, the Squire eventually arrived in a great fluster, with a red face and drooping whiskers.

The crowd hushed. They could tell something was wrong.

'Hrrumph!' the Squire began. 'Mistresses, maids and fellows, my friends . . . um . . . after looking up the right and proper knighting ceremony,' he said, 'I'm afraid Mrs Squire and I have come upon a bit of a hitch.' He twiddled his whiskers apologetically.'

The puzzled villagers pushed forward to hear.

'It seems . . . that is . . . the rules say . . . um . . . well . . . that only a King can make a knight!'

Everyone gasped, except Digory who breathed a huge sigh of relief. *Saved at the last minute!* he thought.

'I'm sorry, Digory,' said Squire Paunch. 'It wouldn't be right and proper, me being only a Squire, I'm afraid.'

The crowd grumbled and booed. They were very disappointed.

But Digory's mother hadn't spent a week making a suit of armour for nothing.

'Only a Squire, my elbow!' she shouted, jumping up on a barrel. 'That's not a problem. Why, we'll make you a King, then you can get on with the knighting.'

With great cheering, the whole village agreed that solved the problem perfectly.

Digory's heart sank again.

'I haven't got much work in the smithy at the moment,' continued Betsy, 'so I can make a crown by Tuesday. But, in the meantime, Arthur's cap will crown you very nicely.'

So, with no further delay, the Squire was crowned King Paunch of Batty-by-Noodle and his first royal duty was to perform the knighthood ceremony.

Digory dismounted and knelt before the King, who struck him gently with a sword on both shoulders.

'Arise, Sir Digory the Dragon Slayer,' he said

solemnly in his royal cap, and everyone cheered and agreed he made a jolly useful King.

The delighted Batty villagers had never had so much to celebrate at once. Minstrels played, maidens danced and everyone tucked into a great feast.

But with the ceremony done, and all the gobbling and gambolling going on, no one noticed Sir Digory, with his lute slung across his back, plod silently away on Barley.

Only one person chased down the lane after Digory, waving a beer flagon in one hand and a bellows in the other.

'Good luck, son!' shouted Betsy happily. 'Go out and have adventures! Fight dragons and marry a princess! And don't forget to oil your joints once a week!'

Chapter Two

KEEPING OUT OF TROUBLE

DIGORY travelled far and wide across the countryside. Although he was used to spending days alone, Digory soon missed his family. Before long he even missed the village boys.

'Nobody told me that being a knight would be so lonely,' he sighed.

Barley whinnied and shook her ragged mane as if she understood.

'We can't go home, Barley, until I've done some good deeds,' explained Digory sadly. 'Maybe we'll find a friend on our adventures . . .'

Meanwhile, there was nothing else to do but search for good deeds and try to avoid dragons, damsels in distress and princesses looking for a husband.

This last task, however, was particularly difficult. Before Digory had travelled far, princesses began to appear all over the place. They jumped out from behind trees and combed their hair at him, or sighed in towers pretending to be damsels in distress. Eventually, Digory realised that princesses hung about *waiting* for knights to come along!

Whenever he met a princess, Digory didn't know what to say. *What do girls talk about?* he asked himself as he climbed off Barley and bowed with a creak.

He thought of his sister Ethelburg. She could spend hours lovingly describing twenty types of mud and how to fling them, so he would try that. But he never met one princess who was the slightest bit interested in mud, or squirrels, or tree houses or dams. Each princess only wished to be admired and told how she was the most wonderful, beautiful, ravishing, gorgeous creature in all the land.

When the princesses just heard mud talk and realised they were not going to be admired at all they would stamp their tiny feet and go off in a huff.

Now, Digory had seen Ethelburg in a mud-flinging fury after losing a match with the Mucky Maidens but *nothing* is as terrifying as a huffy princess.

Before long poor Digory was much more afraid of meeting a princess than of meeting a dragon!

Luckily, Digory the Dragon Slayer had never met a dragon. Whenever he saw a wisp of smoke curling above the treetops he would turn

CASTLE

DRAWBRIDGE

about and ride in the opposite direction, just in case it was the sign of a dragon's fiery breath. *No point in taking any chances*, he'd say to himself. *I don't want to give Barley a fright!*

THEN ONE MORNING . . .

One morning, as Digory plodded along a leafy lane, squeaking gently and humming to himself, he heard a sudden rumble of thunder. Digory looked at the sky but there wasn't a rain cloud in sight. Then the ground shook and flames shot high above the trees ahead.

'A dragon!' cried Digory in alarm. He jumped off Barley and led her about turn. Then, clambering on again he gave the old horse a giddy-up kick.

'I think I'll ride north this morning,' he said out loud in case anyone was watching. (After all, knights are supposed to ride *towards* dragons, not in the opposite direction.)

And with a snort Barley trotted off.

To the north was a castle on a hill with white turret towers and an orchard below. There was no sign of a dragon and no princesses to be seen anywhere. *That looks pretty safe*, thought Digory who, by now, was feeling hungry.

So he trotted up the hill to the castle, with his dragon's tooth glinting in the sun, trying to look bold and brave and knightly.

As Digory rode across the moat and through the castle gate, he noticed everything had a sign with its name written on: 'Drawbridge', 'Wall', 'Courtyard'. Even the people had tickets pinned to their backs: 'Jester', 'Watchman' and 'Dungeon Keeper'.

Digory was greeted by an old man with a quill pen behind his ear, wearing a label saying 'Labeller'.

'Please, tell me, why does everything have a sign?' asked Digory, after giving his full title.

The Labeller groaned as he hunted in his cart for a very long ticket.

'It's His Majesty,' he explained, sharpening the quill pen. 'King Widget has a very bad memory for the names of things. He can remember dates, he never forgets anyone's birthday, but he gets a bit woolly when it comes to names.

'Once he took all morning to remember that his blue-cosy-things were called 'slippers', and couldn't get out of bed until the Queen had guessed what he wanted. It made things very slow, you see. So, now everything is labelled – including you!'

And he produced a long sign that read 'Sir Digory the Dragon Slayer', and an old one just saying 'Horse' for Barley.

DIGORY MEETS KING WIDGET

Once he was labelled, Digory could be presented to the King. This happened whenever a knight arrived at a castle. Digory wished he could be presented to the baker or the muffin man first, but no, knightly business always had to come before food.

King Widget was in the throne room playing marbles.

Digory introduced himself.

'Do you have any good deeds that need doing, Sire?' he asked politely.

'Well, it's very kind of you to offer, my fellow,' said the King with a smile. 'You arrived just at the right moment. As a matter of fact the . . . er . . . the . . . um . . .' he scratched his head and look puzzled. 'Oh, you know, the, the . . . what's it called?'

Digory couldn't begin to guess what the King was trying to remember.

'I'm afraid I don't know, Your Majesty,' he said patiently (thinking to himself in dismay that it might be some time before he saw a muffin or leg of chicken).

'Oh, botherations,' said the King, getting into a terrible fluster.

Then, to Digory's astonishment, the King began to walk slowly up and down the throne room, curtseying to nobody at all and holding out his hand to be kissed.

'Now you know, don't you?' called out the King hopefully, 'It's the grand-giggly-wimple . . .'

'Ah, you mean the Queen, Your Majesty?' suggested Digory.

'Yes, yes, thank you,' said the King. 'Queen, Queen, I *must* remember that word,' he muttered to himself. 'Anyway, where was I? Oh yes, the Queen and I made a list this morning of little jobs to be done around the castle.' And he pulled a long scroll of parchment from a pocket inside his cloak.

Digory looked at it in dismay.

'I was going to make a start on these this afternoon,' explained the King. 'But if you have nothing better to do I'd be terribly grateful.'

Digory thanked the King. At the top of the list was written:

1. Rescue cook's cat.

And so he went off to find the kitchen.

Digory didn't take long to find the castle kitchen for a delicious smell of freshly baked bread led him there by nose. In the middle of a busy bustle of baking was the cook, up to her apron strings in puddings and piecrust. Digory stood in the doorway, gazing at the trays of golden loaves. How he wished to say, 'Please may I have . . .' But, sadly, he swallowed hard.

'Is there a cat to be rescued?' he asked.

'Ooh, my little Pumpkin!' exclaimed the cook. She waved her arms excitedly, dusting everyone with a shower of flour. 'Follow me, Sir Knight.'

The cook took Digory out into the kitchen garden, past fruit bushes and beehives to the orchard, where a tiny, frightened kitten was wedged in the crook of an apple tree.

'There's my little Pumpkin,' sobbed the cook. 'She's been up there since Wednesday. She won't even come down for a saucer of milk.'

Digory, of course, could climb a tree as nimbly

as a squirrel. Up he went and saw at once
what was the problem.

'Her label is snagged on a branch,' he called
down softly. Digory reached up and released
Pumpkin. To his delight she tumbled into his
arms and licked his face gratefully.

The cook was so pleased to have her kitten
safe once more she took Digory back to the
kitchen, laid a cloth on the table and served
him a huge dish of mutton stew and
dumplings.

When Digory had finished his third helping the rest of King Widget's list didn't look so bad.

So Digory set about doing good deeds around the castle. First he polished the King's armour, then he chopped down an old tree in the orchard that was about to fall on some damsons. When that was done he unblocked the well, fishing out two rusty pails, a pair of breeches, a frying pan and a chamber pot.

All afternoon Digory mended this and fixed

that. By teatime he was hungry and tired but very pleased with his work. The last deed on the King's list was to put a new handle on the muffin man's bell, for which Digory was given a basket of muffins and currant buns to take on his way. But Digory could not leave without performing two more knightly duties. He found King Widget licking his fingers in the kitchen garden beneath a weather-beaten sign saying 'Figs'.

Just One Last Thing . . .

'Well done, Sir Knight,' said the King gratefully when he heard that all the good deeds had been done. 'Now what may I do for you in return?'

'I don't need anything, Sire, except some hay for my horse,' replied Digory. 'But first I must ask if you have any damsels in distress here that need to be saved?' Digory crossed his fingers behind his back, hoping all the damsels in the land were happily having tea at that moment.

But the King nodded. 'Oh, yes, we've got hundreds of them here.'

Digory couldn't believe his ears.

'They were all going to make jam, you see,' the King continued. 'But wait a minute . . .' He stopped and looked at Digory suspiciously. 'Your memory must be as bad as mine. The damsons *were* in distress until you chopped that tree down in the orchard. Don't you see, you've already saved them, my friend!' And he offered Digory a fig.

Digory breathed a sigh of relief. He had been horrified at the idea of saving a hundred damsels in distress with jam! He decided not to mention damsels again, but there was still the little matter of marrying a princess.

Digory had seen no sign at all of a princess in the castle of King Widget. No combs in the well, no lost silk slippers in the orchard. So he was certain he would soon be safely on his way with the basket of muffins.

'I don't suppose you have any daughters, Your Majesty?' he said quietly from behind his fig, hoping the King wouldn't even hear.

'Oh dear, I thought you might ask that,' sighed the King. 'Yes, I have just one daughter. Her name is Enid.'

Digory's heart sank into his tin boots and his tummy rumbled loudly in protest.

The King unpeeled another fig thoughtfully and beckoned Digory close.

'I know you knights are always looking for a princess to marry but I'm afraid Enid is not the usual sort of princess,' he explained in a low voice. 'To be honest she's quiet and plain and *unusual*, Sir Digory,' he said. 'She won't sit in a tower all day combing her long, golden, um . . .'

'Hair?' suggested Digory.

'Ah, yes, hair!' the King smiled gratefully. 'She won't comb her long, golden hair all day like the other girls. The truth is, she doesn't even *have* long, golden hair. It's sort of mud brown and sticks up like . . . er . . .'

'Crested waves?' Digory offered. 'Angel's curls?'

The King made a snouty sort of face and wiggled his fingers about on top of his head. 'Sticks up, Diggers, sticks up like a . . . a hodgepig, you see! And, I must tell you, she won't stay in a tower either. She prefers to climb those twiggy things with leaves and play the crumhorn all day. In fact, she would

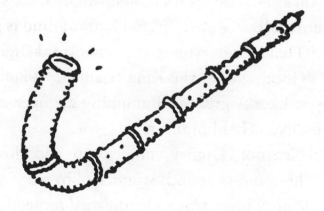

much rather talk to badgers and squirrels than any bold, brave knight.'

The King blushed uncomfortably. 'Nevertheless we love her, you hear. For all we know, she may just be ahead of fashion with her hairstyle.' He set his crown straight. 'It was proper knightly of you to ask, Sir Digory. I know that's what you chaps are supposed to do. But I don't expect she's the sort of princess you're looking for.'

The King took Digory's arm and began to walk him back through the garden into the yard where Barley was tethered.

'Maybe I could do you a good deal on a . . . you know, clip-clop-nosebag-whatsit,' he said hopefully.

'That sounds wonderful to me,' said Digory.

'Good, good,' the King beamed. 'What do you like? A great, gallumphing galloper or a pretty, piebald prancer?'

'No, no!' Digory jumped up and down. 'The *princess* sounds wonderful to me . . .'

King Widget was so astonished to hear this that he stepped backwards and fell into the horse trough!

PRINCESS ENID

As the stable boys pulled dripping King Widget on to his feet Digory explained.

'All the other princesses are so beautiful and grand, Your Highness, I never know what to say to them. You see, I'm a blacksmith's son. I've never really wanted to meet a princess at all.'

'Quite sensible, old chap,' nodded the King, wringing out his beard. 'They're a huffy lot these days.'

'But, Your Majesty, I like to climb twiggy things with leaves and play the lute, and I would much rather talk to badgers and squirrels too!' declared Digory boldly.

'You would?' said King Widget in amazement. 'You like doing the very same things?' The King looked thoughtful and Digory suddenly felt very shy.

'Well, you've worked hard doing good deeds for me all day,' the King smiled kindly at Digory. 'Tomorrow we're having um . . . a . . .

a grass-in-the-sandwiches, you know . . .?'

'A picnic!' cried Digory.

'Yes, exactly, a picnic. Come and meet Enid then.'

And so it was arranged.

That night, Digory composed a song for Enid, with a special crumhorn chorus for her to play. At last here was someone who liked the same things as him. For the first time Digory realised that he'd never had a friend. He was so excited he couldn't sleep. So he sat in the moonlit courtyard on a sack of straw and played his lute to Barley all night long. Barley slept happily through every note, dreaming of soft ripe pears.

THE PICNIC

The next day Barley's dream came true. The picnic was held in the orchard under trees marked 'Pear'.

Digory arrived in his freshly oiled armour. He found the King playing leapfrog with a lady labelled 'Queen' but no princess anywhere.

Digory felt disappointed and shy again. *She probably heard my singing last night and is hiding somewhere with a basket on her head*, he thought sadly.

He remembered how the village boys used to tease him about his ginger hair and lanky legs and long sausage nose. *How silly to think Enid would want to meet me*, he told himself.

Then suddenly a pear dropped on his head,

and another. Digory looked up. There, sitting in the tree above, was a girl with brown hair sticking up like a hodgepig, balancing a crumhorn on her knee.

Digory didn't need to read her label to know that this was Princess Enid!

'Come on up, Sir Digory,' said Enid, 'there's room for two.'

Well, I won't bother to tell you everything that happened next. Enid had heard how Digory saved the cook's cat and how he'd done so many good deeds for her father. Before long they were lost in lute and crumhorn talk, with plenty of laughing and turnip pasties. Enid knew all about music and animals and trees, and had many of the very same thoughts that Digory had himself.

'I've never met anyone like you, Digory,' she smiled.

Digory thought of King Paunch's knighting ceremony and Barley the carthorse and Betsy's homemade armour.

'I expect I'm not like the usual knights that come here,' he said.

'But I like you *because* you're different,' said the princess. 'Lots of knights come to our castle, striding around, boasting of how strong and brave they are, talking about adventures and dangerous deeds. None of them would be gentle enough to rescue a cat, and we never become friends because they're far too busy galloping around the moat to sit and talk to me.'

'Oh, I'd like to talk to you best of all,' said Digory, 'and I can't gallop anywhere!' he added truthfully.

'Good!' said Enid. And, by the time the picnic was finished, Digory and the princess had become friends.

CAN IT BE TRUE?

So, Digory stayed at King Widget's castle all summer. He and Princess Enid spent happy hours building tree houses in the woods, playing duets, having picnics and thinking thoughts together.

Enid showed Digory where badgers lived and he showed her how to dam a stream and make a stick bridge.

On Saturdays Digory did good deeds for the King and, on Sunday afternoons, Enid pretended to be a damsel in distress and Digory saved her.

Then, one afternoon, King Widget sent for him from the throne room. There the Queen and the princess sat looking serious and solemn.

Oh dear, thought Digory, *no one is smiling. Have I done something wrong?* He tried to guess what it might be. He'd done a few things that were not quite right the week before, and a couple of things that should have been done in a different sort of way and one difficult thing that he'd given up in the middle. But none of these were as serious as the King's stern face.

'Are you happy here, Digory?' began the Queen.

'Oh yes,' replied Digory, 'very happy, Your Highness.'

'You have been with us now a long time, Sir Knight,' said the King stroking his beard thoughtfully, 'and we are pleased to see your friendship with the . . . um . . . um . . . you know . . . the spiky-tra-la-la . . .' Enid turned so that her father could see her label. 'Ah, yes, Enid. That's it, my darling. Pretty name, pretty name . . .'

The Queen coughed to remind the King to get back to business. Digory had a heavy feeling in his heart.

'Well now, the thing is, we never had a boy of our own,' the King continued, 'and you've been like a son to us this summer. We'd miss you frightfully if you went off to do good deeds anywhere else . . .'

Digory knew the next word would be 'but'.

'So,' said the King, 'we would like you to stay with us and be our prince – you'd make a jolly good one.'

Digory thought he must have misheard the King. He was so astonished that he couldn't reply.

The King bent close to whisper in his ear.

'Actually, it was Enid's idea,' he said. 'Don't disappoint her, Diggers. We all want you to stay.'

Digory still couldn't speak, but he nodded his head again and again until Enid pinched the end of his nose.

'Your silly head will drop off, Prince Digory!' she laughed. 'Let's go and celebrate with some fireworks!'

And that was that.

NOT QUITE . . .

Well, of course, that is never really that, you know, especially in stories – there is always *something else . . .*

Chapter Three

HAVE WE FORGOTTEN SOMETHING?

DIGORY was thrilled to be able to stay with his best friend, Enid. He wasn't sure if he wanted to become a prince, but he was certainly glad he'd no longer have to roam aimlessly around looking for damsels and dragons and chivalrousness. *I'll write to my mother straightaway*, he thought to himself, *and tell her I am going to live happily ever after. Maybe she will come to visit.*

But just as Digory sharpened his quill pen, King Widget knocked on his door.

'Sorry to disturb you, old chap,' said the King, scratching his head. 'There's a small thing I seem to have forgotten.'

Digory hoped this thing wasn't going to take as long to remember as the pair of slippers.

'There is something I had to ask you . . .' King Widget mumbled.

'Was it about lutes?' guessed Digory hopefully.

But the King had completely forgotten and couldn't give him a clue. Digory suggested everything he could think of from A to Z but still the King was stuck, so they sent for the Queen and Enid. Together everyone tried to jog the King's memory.

'Did you want to know his crown size, dear?' suggested the Queen.

'Or maybe you wanted to play noughts and crosses?' tried Enid.

But the King shook his head firmly. It definitely wasn't anything to do with crowns or criss-cross. The chamberlain was summoned and the jester too. Even the cook tried to guess what the King had forgotten. They guessed all afternoon until way past teatime. It was *much worse* than the slippers.

'Well, what *sort* of thing was it, dear?' sighed the Queen, who'd been taking a bath when the King called and could feel a sneeze coming on.

'Something . . . something to do with . . . snails, I think . . .' said the King at last. Then suddenly he laughed. 'Of course, silly old buffer! It wasn't anything really important, sorry everyone.'

They all sighed with relief.

'It wasn't snails, it was *scales*!' laughed the King. 'I had just forgotten to tell Digory here about the dragon!'

THE UNIMPORTANT THING

'I'd just forgotten to say that, as he is going to become our prince, he will have to slay the dragon,' said King Widget. 'It's the usual knightly thing. No problem for a dragon slayer like yourself.'

Digory went weak at the knees and had to sit down.

'But . . . but . . . but . . .' he stammered, like a dripping drip.

'Aaatishoo!' interrupted the damp Queen. 'What a lot of guessing over a dragon!' and she shivered off to her bath.

Digory took a deep breath.

'Which . . . particular dragon might that be, Your Highness?' he asked feebly, as his voice came back.

'There's a dragon in a cave at the edge of our forest,' explained the King. 'He's called the Horrible Gnasher Toast'em Firebreath. Now that you are going to be our prince you won't mind killing the dragon, will you?

Otherwise we shall have to find another knight, which seems rather silly as we have you here.'

'We think there's only one dragon,' said Enid.

'Quite right, my dear,' said the King, shaking Digory's hand. 'There's probably only one . . . at least there aren't usually more than two, don't you find? Well, anyway, kill 'em all, that's the best thing. Now, anyone for a glass of . . . you know . . . gives-you-the-giggles?'

And that really was that.

THE USUAL KNIGHTLY THING

Poor Digory the Dragon Slayer walked round the battlements wondering what to do. He had never felt more troubled in his life. He wished with all his heart he could just be plain Digory again – poking sticks in the stream in Batty-by-Noodle woods, not having to be brave or *shiverous* or fight jaw-dripping, flesh-ripping, bone-crunching, snout-snarling, bloodthirsty dragons.

But then he thought of Enid. If he went back home now he would always be lonely without her. And when he thought about Enid something strange happened – Digory began to feel a tiny bit brave. So, he thought about her some more. He thought about her very hard, all afternoon, and by teatime he felt nearly stout-hearted, by suppertime he was almost daring and by bedtime he was fearless enough to decide that there was nothing else to do but slay the dragon.

However, the next morning at breakfast, when Digory announced that he was going off to slay the dragon, nobody took much notice at all. Enid gave Digory her portrait picture and a handkerchief, and the King gave him a map of the Kingdom. Then they went back to their porridge. They assumed Digory the Dragon Slayer had done this sort of thing so many times before that he'd be back in time for lunch.

So Digory, who'd been hoping for a bit of a fuss and a hero's goodbye, didn't even get a bacon sandwich.

'It seems to me,' Digory said to Barley as he fetched her saddle, 'that sometimes people make a terrible fuss when you don't want them to, and sometimes they don't make a fuss when you wish they would.'

But this sort of thought was far too difficult for Barley, who didn't hear it anyway.

So, with a heavy heart and an empty stomach, Digory set off to slay the Horrible Gnasher Toast'em Firebreath.

Chapter Four

A Little Detour

DIGORY and Barley plodded out of the valley and up the hill, then down the hill and through the cornfields. Then up another hill, through a dark forest and down the other side again.

Digory grew cold and hungry. The clouds swelled dark and grey. They seemed to soak up all his bravery like a sponge. Digory thought of the King and Queen and Enid playing marbles in front of the fire.

Then he thought of his mother in the smithy, laughing as the sparks flew off her anvil, while Arthur, Tom and Ethelburg roasted chestnuts in the furnace.

Poor Digory felt forgotten and *shiverous* from the top of his cold helmet down to his chilly tin boots.

Eventually he came to a hazel wood where nuts and blackberries grew. He stopped to eat and gave Barley a humbug. Then he remembered the King's map in his pocket.

Digory unrolled the map and studied the kingdom of King Widget. It looked rather hurriedly drawn, with the castle sketched in the middle and Gnasher's cave marked by a red cross. Ten leagues to the south of the dragon's cave, Digory noticed a blue squiggle. Looking closer he discovered it was a dolphin's head rising out of a curly wave. It was the sea.

Now, Digory had never seen the sea. He'd heard songs and stories about it. He had seen cockles and crabs at the market. But he'd always wondered what the sea was really like.

A small, tempting thought started to murmur in Digory's head. *You never said exactly when you were going to slay the dragon,* the thought whispered. *No one would notice if you took a long route and went to the sea on your way,* it went on enticingly. *And then you never know, the dragon might even have gone away by the time you come back . . .*

Suddenly, a commotion of rooks croaked loudly overhead. They seemed to screech, 'Jaw-dripping, flesh-ripping, bone-crunching, snout-snarling, bloodthirsty dragon!'

That decided it.

'We're going to the sea,' Digory told Barley. 'We might slay the dragon when we get back!'

TO THE SEA

Digory studied the King's map and calculated that they should reach the sea by teatime. So they rode through the wood and over the hill. Through the valley and across the hump-back bridge. Then along the river and into another wood.

As they plodded on their way Digory, now in much better spirits, composed a song which went like this:

'*Down to the briny sea we go,*
Where dolphins swim and blue whales
blow,
And shipwrecks creak on the rocks below.
Ho heigh, fishy tails, heigh ho!'

But what about Enid, you ask? Well, this is the story of Digory and so it is the story of what Digory did. Remember, he wasn't a great hero at the beginning, just an ordinary sort of every day, stream-poking chap like you or me. Sometimes we do a good thing, sometimes a bad thing, and sometimes people mistake us for heroes and expect us to fight dragons.

Anyway, Digory decided he would rather paddle in the sea than slay the Horrible Gnasher Toast'em Firebreath and I wonder what you would have done?

Meanwhile, Barley didn't know or care where she was going but she knew she needed a scratch. So, spotting a useful bramble with plenty of thorns she stopped. Digory, puzzling over the map as he rode, fell off headfirst into the bush.

'I don't understand,' he said, rubbing his dented helmet. 'We should have reached the sea by now.'

'Aha! Gadzooks!' cried a voice in alarm. 'A talking bush! Be silent at once. Don't put a spell on me, enchanted spirit.'

Digory peered through the brambles and saw a young man about his own age wearing a tall, crumpled hat and a ragged black cloak.

'Help!' said Digory. 'I'm not a spirit. I'm stuck.'

'How do I *know* that you're not a magic spirit, hiding in a bush?' asked the ragged man suspiciously.

Digory thought about this. In fact he wasn't quite sure how he got to be in a bush to start with.

'Well, if I *was* a magic spirit I could get myself out,' he replied. 'So give me a hand.' And he stuck his gauntlet through the brambles.

The ragged man pulled Digory out.

'I'm a wizard myself, actually,' he announced, straightening his hat. 'Burdock at your service.'

Digory had never met a wizard before but something about Burdock didn't seem quite right.

'I thought wizards were supposed to be all-powerful, not scared of talking bushes?' he said.

'I wasn't scared,' Burdock said with a

scowl. 'Anyway, I'll prove to you that I'm a wizard. What will you give me if I tell your fortune?'

Now, although Digory didn't quite believe that Burdock was a wizard he was very interested to hear his fortune. There were many things he would like to know. Would he ever find the sea? Would the dragon be gone from the Kingdom of King Widget one day? Would he ever see Enid again?

'I don't have much,' said Digory, 'but if you can tell my fortune I'll give you anything I have.'

Barley snorted loudly.

'Except my horse, that is,' Digory added just in time, wondering whether Barley might be able to read his lips after all.

Burdock swung his tattered cloak about him like great raven's wings and shut his eyes. Then slowly he stretched out his arm and pointed a finger at Digory.

Digory suddenly changed his mind but it was too late.

'I shall begin.' Burdock said in a deep slow voice. And he began:

'Through the countryside you roam,
Many leagues away from home.
Twice were struck by noble sword,
Yet no wound have you endured.
Now you hunt for dragon's lair,
And what fate awaits you there.'

Digory listened in amazement. How did Burdock know King Paunch had struck Digory on both shoulders without a wound? How did he know he was far from home? How did he know about Gnasher? Only a wizard could see into the past like this, for certain.

'But what about the future?' Digory asked.

Wizard Burdock shut his eyes and pulled his cloak above his head. Slowly he spoke again:

'In your name my eyes do see,
There the magic letter 'g'.
So fear not what lies ahead,
Banish all your darkest dread.

I hear music, I hear laughter,
You'll live happily ever after.'

'Is that it?' said Digory.

'Yup,' said Burdock. 'That's usually enough for most people.'

'No mention of the sea then?' Digory enquired.

'Nope,' said Burdock.

Digory looked very disappointed, so Burdock shut his eyes again and stretched out his pointing finger.

'Ah, yes,' he continued in his fortune-telling voice.

'There *is* something sloshy in your future – not the sea exactly, maybe a pond or a puddle . . . it's very slimy and it's very dark . . .' He paused and frowned. 'I'm afraid I can't see any more. Everything's grown dim.'

'A slimy, dark puddle!' Digory cried in dismay. 'That's not very exciting. Who ever heard of a knight having an adventure in a slimy, dark puddle?'

'Well, you wanted to know,' said Burdock sounding rather hurt. 'Now, what will you give me in return for my fortune-telling?' He began to rifle through Barley's saddlebags.

But Digory was busy pondering over the wizard's words.

'We were on our way to the sea, you see,' he puzzled aloud. 'If the map is right we *should* be sitting in a sand dune at this very moment.'

Burdock stopped his rummaging to take a look.

'There's nothing wrong with the map,' he said, turning it upside down. 'But I don't think you know your north and south. The sea is ten leagues away. We are here . . .' He pointed to a spot just a flea's footstep away from Gnasher's cave!

SURPRISE, SURPRISE!

Digory couldn't believe his eyes. Had they really been travelling around in circles since breakfast? How did they manage to arrive at the only place on the map Digory *didn't* want to visit?

'Your dragon's cave is just behind that bush,' said Burdock helpfully. 'I'd like to hang around and watch. I've never seen anyone battle with a jaw-dripping, flesh-ripping, bone-crunching, snout-snarling, bloodthirsty dragon before. But I've got to feed my bats at sunset so I must get home.'

Digory thought this was probably turning out to be the most awful day of his life.

'By the way,' said the wizard, 'you agreed I could have anything I wanted if I told your fortune, so I'll just take this.' And he strapped Digory's lute across his back.

That was the last straw. Now it definitely *was* the most awful day of Digory's life, and there was still a dragon to slay before bed-time.

'Cheer up,' said Burdock, when he saw Digory's long face. 'Remember, *I see dancing, I see laughter. You'll live happily ever after.*

Take this magic sword, I don't need it much. You might find it useful.' And, leaving his battered old sword behind, Burdock the Wizard hurried off into the woods.

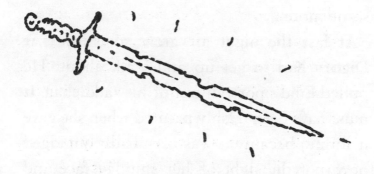

Digory felt lonelier than ever when Burdock had gone. He picked up the sword. It didn't look magic. It didn't twitch in his hand or shoot sparks from the hilt. Still, it seemed as if fate had decided Digory was going to have to face the Horrible Gnasher Toast'em Firebreath and he would need all the help he could get, magic or not, so he tucked it into his belt.

After some thought Digory decided the best

time, in fact the *only* time to visit a dragon must be while it was asleep. So he waited until dusk, and then when night fell and the moon came out shining its eerie beams into the mouth of the dragon's cave he waited some more . . .

At last the night air grew so chilly that Digory had to get up and walk about. He pulled Enid's portrait out of his saddlebag. It must have been freshly painted when she gave it to him because it was very badly smudged now, but the sight of her smudgy face and hodgepig hair made him feel braver, so he tucked it inside his armour for luck. Barley ambled over and nuzzled Digory's ear as if she knew something was going to happen, as if she wanted to give her little bit of encouragement too.

'Goodbye, my friend,' said Digory. 'I expect I shall never return from this adventure. If I am not back by morning you must go home to Batty-by-Noodle without me.'

However, if Barley really could read

Digory's lips she only paid attention to the last few words and, turning clumsily about, walked off with a snort into the night.

Poor Digory was left to face the Horrible Gnasher Toast'em Firebreath alone. He wanted his lute, he wanted his friend Enid, he wanted his mother. He would even have been pleased to see his sister Ethelburg at that moment. She'd be a good match for a dragon. But there really was no turning back this time. Digory lit a torch, gripped the hilt of Burdock's magic sword and slowly stepped inside the cave.

Chapter Five

THE FATE AWAITS

THE dragon's cave was horribly cold and clammy.

This must be shiverous, thought Digory, *and I don't like it!* He also didn't like the tummy-churning stench of rotten meat and the spooky echo of water dripping in deep, dark caverns.

Digory held the torch before him and stepped slowly through the winding tunnel. With each step he knew he was closer to the dragon, and further away from escape. The tunnel sloped down and then opened out into a chamber as large as King Widget's banqueting hall. *This must be where the dragon devours his prey*, Digory thought nervously. But there weren't any bones to be seen – just a heap of colourful stuff lying by a rock. When Digory looked closer he discovered it was a pile of maiden's cloaks and jewellery, shoes and crowns. He went weak at the knees.

'This is only his cloakroom,' he said with a shudder. 'And I don't think any of these guests will be leaving!'

Suddenly a sharp draught blew through a crevice in the rock and put out his torch! Digory stood very still. All around him there was darkness and somewhere ahead of him was darkness with a dragon in it, *or maybe two.*

His bravery fizzled out like the flame.

'No one can be expected to fight a d-d-dragon in the d-d-dark,' he said to himself, trying to stay calm. 'No one could complain if I t-t-turned around now and went b-b-back.'

But which was the way b-b-back? Digory crawled about on the knees of his tin suit, trying to find the tunnel entrance. When he reached a cave wall he stood up and took a few steps forward. It felt like the tunnel b-b-back, but it was really . . .

THE TUNNEL TO THE D-D-DRAGON'S LAIR!

As Digory stumbled blindly through the cave, the rotten smell grew stronger and a clatter of small rocks fell ahead. Just as he was starting to suspect this was not the tunnel b-b-back after all, a terrifying snort sent more rocks tumbling at his feet. The jaw-dripping, flesh-

ripping, bone-crunching, snout-snarling, bloodthirsty dragon must be there in the darkness ahead – but where?

Poor Digory was petrified. He shuddered and shook until his armour rattled like a tinker's cart. The sound filled the cave with a deafening echo.

Then the dragon spoke.

'WHAT GREAT ARMY OF KNIGHTS COMES TO MY CAVE?' his deep voice boomed.

In an instant, Digory realised that the dragon could not see him in the dark. He shook his tin leggings and sure enough they sounded like a hundred knights shuffling impatiently. Digory felt a little braver. 'If only I can fool this dragon,' he said to himself, 'I might get a chance to escape.'

So he took a deep breath and imagined he was Ethelburg playing let's pretend.

'I am Sir Digory the Dragon Slayer,' he shouted sternly, 'and I come here with my army to slay the Horrible Gnasher Toast'em

Firebreath, and . . . er . . . anyone else who crosses my path.'

The dragon was silent. Digory heard the scratching and scuffling of clawed feet.

'WHY SHOULD I BE AFRAID OF YOU, SIR DIGORY? THESE JAWS OF MINE HAVE SNAPPED OFF THE HEADS OF A THOUSAND KNIGHTS.'

Digory swallowed hard. He tried with all his might to imagine that there *were* a thousand knights behind him.

'You *should* be afraid, dragon,' he replied, 'because these are the fiercest knights in the land.' He rattled his armour for effect. 'One of them slayed the Great King Troll and another killed a two-headed sea serpent with his bare hands.' Digory was quite pleased with this. Making up stories was just like making up songs.

The dragon grunted, as if deciding whether to believe him or not. But Digory was just beginning to enjoy himself. He found it easy to imagine things in the dark.

'All my knights carry magic swords,' he continued. 'They can change any creature to stone with just one strike. I, myself, have slain one hundred mountain lions with a catapult while wrestling with the Ferocious Four Fanged Beast of Batty Woods, single-handed.'

Now Digory was really feeling the part. He slapped his thigh with his gauntlet and it made a deafening clatter.

'WELL, I HAVE THE BONES OF A HUNDRED THOUSAND KNIGHTS FOR MY BED,' boasted the dragon. 'MY NOSE IS AS KEEN AS THE WIND AND MY EYES ARE SHARPER THAN THE EYES OF AN EAGLE. MY CLAWS CAN RIP DOWN CASTLE WALLS AND MY LONG TONGUE MAY PICK A JUICY MAIDEN FROM HER BED. AND WHEN I HAVE DEVOURED MY FILL I DRINK THE FIRE OF VOLCANOES FOR MY THIRST.'

But this did not frighten Digory, now standing proudly at the head of a great army.

'Ha! What good are your eagle eyes against a wizard's spell?' he jeered. 'I have twenty wizards in my army who will make gruesome spirits appear before your eyes and tie your tongue into a knot that may never be undone. At my command they will turn your claws into ribbons and your keen nose into a pumpkin.'

'BUT I HAVE SET ALIGHT GREAT FORESTS WITH MY BREATH!' bellowed the dragon.

Digory the Invincible laughed. 'And I have the teeth of a hundred dragons on my helmet!'

As he listened to the booming echo of his own words Digory felt as fearless as a true knight. He drew Burdock's sword from its scabbard and the sound of a hundred swords drawn echoed through the cave.

But, as Digory took one step forward into the darkness, he heard a small, whimpering snivel.

'Oh, please don't harm me. I'm only small

really,' sobbed a trembling voice. 'I haven't been telling the truth. I can't really tear down castle walls with my claws. I've never even seen a castle. In fact, I'm still so young that my claws aren't even grown yet.'

Digory, who'd worked himself up into a great state of heroic chivalrousness, felt suddenly disappointed.

'You mean you *aren't* a jaw-dripping, flesh-ripping, bone-crunching, snout-snarling, bloodthirsty dragon after all?' he said in amazement.

'Oh, no, Sire,' snivelled the dragon. 'The jaw-ripping, snout-thirsty one is Horrible Gnasher, my father. This evening we set off on my first hunting trip, but I got lost in the woods. I found my way home and now I'm waiting for him to return. He's going to be so angry when he gets back. He'll be really mad. Really, horribly, blood-spittingly, bone-gnashingly furious.'

Digory heard the little dragon sniff his tears away and suddenly felt ashamed of himself.

His father had always brought him up to tell the truth and here he was telling dragon-sized porkie-pasties in order to trick a poor creature who'd never done him any harm.

'Quick,' cried the dragon in a trembling voice, 'I can hear my father's great wings beating over the woods. You'd better flee with your army of knights before he scorches you all to cinders!'

Digory didn't need to think twice about the dragon's advice. 'Thank you for your warning,' he said. 'I shall go, but first I must tell you that I haven't been telling the truth either. I'm not really big and fierce,' he said. 'I'm just one boy alone, who doesn't know how to slay a sausage. My army of knights was only an echo. I'm very sorry that I frightened you.'

'Oh, that makes me feel *much* better,' said the dragon, sounding happier. 'I'm not afraid now I know that you are only one boy, alone.' He coughed and cleared his throat. 'Let me give you some light to help you on your way . . .'

Suddenly there was a deafening roar and a jet of flame shot across the cave, lighting Digory's torch and revealing not a small, trembling, little dragon but AN ENORMOUS JAW-DRIPPING, FLESH-RIPPING, BONE-CRUNCHING, SNOUT-SNARLING, BLOODTHIRSTY DRAGON AFTER ALL!!

HEEEEEEEELLLLLP!

'TRIED TO TRICK ME, EH?' hissed the Horrible Gnasher Toast'em Firebreath, rolling his red eyes.

'Well, you tried to t-t-trick me t-t-too,' stuttered Digory, horrified.

'YES, BUT I TRICKED YOU BETTER!' the dragon replied with a nasty, drooling smile. 'AND NOW ALL THIS TRICKING HAS MADE ME HUNGRY SO I'M GOING TO GNAW THE FLESH OFF YOUR SKINNY BONES FOR BREAKFAST.'

Digory suddenly remembered to be terrified. His hair stood on end, his teeth chattered, his knees knocked, his blood ran cold and his legs turned to jelly. *This was it. This was* chivalrous *and Digory knew it was going to be the last feeling he would ever have.*

The dragon crept slowly towards Digory, like a cat ready to pounce . . .

Digory had one thought. *Would it be better to blow out the light and be gobbled up in the dark, or to start running away and be gobbled up from behind?*

Gnasher stopped close enough for Digory to feel the heat from his charred nostrils and smell his rotten breath. The dragon eyed him up and down.

'I ALWAYS PREFER MY LITTLE TIT-BITS PEELED,' he said with a gruesome grin. 'I FIND ARMOUR SOMETIMES STICKS IN THE THROAT. WILL YOU REMOVE IT OR SHALL I?'

Digory began to pull off his gloves obediently when the dragon opened his mouth to lick his lips. With amazement Digory saw that the Horrible Gnasher Toast'em Firebreath had no teeth! There, inside his gruesome snout was a pair of gums as pink as a baby's bottom!

Digory couldn't help himself – he started to giggle! His fear of being crunched and chewed by razor sharp fangs suddenly dissolved into uncontrollable laughter. He laughed and laughed and laughed until he got the hiccups.

'Who's afraid of being sucked to death by a toothless . . . hic . . . dragon!' he chortled.

'Who's afraid of a . . . toothless dragon!' echoed a hundred sneering voices out of the darkness.

The Horrible Gnasher was completely taken aback. No one had ever laughed at him before. He shrank against the wall of the cave, confused for a moment.

In an instant, Digory saw that he had a chance. With a flourish he drew Burdock's sword once more and sliced the air like a true knight.

'Stay back, toothless dragon!' he cried. 'This is a magic sword and I shall turn you into a newt!'

The dragon didn't want to be turned into a tincey, tiny, slimy thing that scrambled around in a pond. He swung about with a *whip-crack* of his tail and roared away down a dark passage, cursing and hissing foul smelling steam.

WHO WANTS A CHANCE TO ESCAPE?

At this point, of course, you or I would have turned tail and run in the opposite direction, as fast as our tin boots could carry us. But Digory was actually beginning to act like a true knight. In fact, Digory was growing into a truer knight with every moment he spent in the Horrible Gnasher's cave, although he didn't notice this himself. Digory didn't think twice. He chased after the dragon, brandishing Burdock's sword along the dark, winding tunnel.

Suddenly there was an ear-splitting avalanche of rocks ahead and billows of dust shot back along the passage. The dragon's roaring had shaken down a rock fall and blocked its escape.

Digory stumbled blindly forward, coughing and spluttering, until he found himself face to face once again with the Horrible Gnasher. The trapped dragon turned and reared angrily. Sparks and cinders sputtered from his flaring nostrils. Digory raised the magic sword high above his head.

'I THOUGHT YOU SAID YOU DIDN'T KNOW HOW TO SLAY A SAUSAGE?' hissed the dragon. 'YOU LIED AGAIN, DID-N'T YOU?'

Digory dithered uncomfortably for a moment, but he wasn't going to be tricked again. If he delayed using the magic sword the dragon would surely fry him with its flaming breath, like a miserable sliver of bacon.

'I'm not going to slay you,' he shouted

through the smoke and dust. 'I'm just going to turn you into a newt, so that you'll never be able to devour anybody again.'

'BUT SOMETHING MIGHT DEVOUR ME!' exclaimed the dragon, and with a terrible roar he drew a deep breath to ignite the flame in his throat.

Digory's chance was running out. He pointed the sword towards Gnasher's head but, to his horror, realised he didn't know what to do next.

'Burdock never told me the magic words!' he gasped.

'BURDOCK?' said Gnasher in surprise, suddenly coughing out his flame. 'BURDOCK – A SNIVELLING RAT IN A TATTERED BLACK CLOAK GAVE YOU THAT SWORD?'

'Um . . . yes,' replied Digory, sensing in an instant that things were about to take a jaw-dripping, flesh-ripping, bone-crunching, snout-snarling, bloodthirsty turn for the worse. 'Burdock the Wizard gave me this magic sword and n-now I shall turn you into a n-n-newt!"

'WELL, IF THAT IS BURDOCK'S SWORD THEN THERE'S MORE MAGIC IN MY ELBOW!' laughed the Horrible Gnasher and, with a flick of his tail, he flung the sword out of Digory's hand and back along the passage.

'YOUR BURDOCK IS NOTHING MORE THAN A COMMON THIEF AND TRICK-STER,' he gloated triumphantly.

'But he told my fortune,' protested Digory (believing in his heart that the dragon was unfortunately telling the truth). 'Burdock knew who I was and what I had come to do.'

Hearing this the dragon narrowed his eyes and slowly stretched his front foot towards Digory, with one hooked claw extended.

Digory froze into a statue of *shiverousness*.

'ANYONE COULD TELL YOUR FOR-TUNE, SIR DIGORY.' Gnasher smiled wide-ly and gently pulled the label on Digory's back round across his chest. There were the words 'Sir Digory the Dragon Slayer' telling all.

Digory's heart dropped with a thud into his boots. So that was how Burdock knew Digory had been struck twice by a sword but not wounded – from the knighting ceremony. And that is how he knew why Digory had come to the forest!

'AND I SUPPOSE HE TOOK SOME-THING FROM YOU AS WELL?' The dragon obviously knew all about the tricks of Burdock's trade.

Digory remembered his precious lute and he felt as glum as a cold suet pudding.

'WELL, NOW I AM GOING TO TAKE SOMETHING FROM YOU TOO, SIR DIGORY THE DRAGON SLAYER – I SHALL HAVE YOUR SCRAWNY FLESH FROM YOUR GRISTLY BONES!' And the dragon picked up Digory by his breeches with one claw and carried him back down the passage to the great chamber. As Digory swung from Gnasher's foot he spotted Burdock's sword among the rocks and with a swipe picked it up.

This may not be magic, he thought miserably to himself, *but I expect a proper knight is always gobbled up with his sword.*

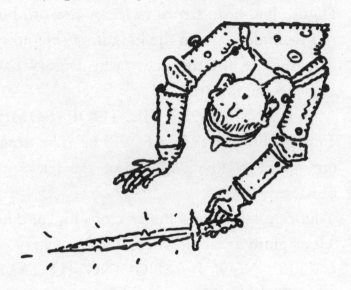

THE TROUBLE WITH TEETH

Now, although Digory had felt suspicious of Burdock from the first moment they met in the bush, he had somehow trusted the wizard's words. 'I hear music, I hear laughter.

You'll live happily ever after.' But here, in his darkest hour, there was not even a trickster's promise to comfort him.

Gnasher carried Digory to the corner of the great chamber and dropped him on to an enormous bed of bones. Digory shuddered! His feet rested on a huge rib cage and a hollow eyed skull stared up at his elbow.

'NOW, WHERE WERE WE? AH YES, YOU WERE REMOVING THAT ARMOUR,' snapped the dragon, licking his scorched lips. 'HELMETS ALWAYS STICK IN MY GUMS.'

Digory did what he was told. He had no bravery left and no more *shiverousness*. He felt so beaten that he didn't care whether the dragon ate him from the back or the front or tossed him up in the air and swallowed him whole. He took off the helmet, with the tooth Betsy had so proudly welded on the top, and laid it beside him on the bones. As the dragon watched closely Digory spotted something in the pile. He reached out and picked up a huge, white thing that was almost as big as the helmet itself.

'THIS WAS THE LAST TOOTH TO GO,' the dragon sighed. 'I CHEWED TOO MANY MAIDENS WEARING BRACE-LETS AND CROWNS. I WAS TOO IMPA-TIENT. THAT WAS THE PROBLEM.'

Digory looked at the tooth on his helmet. Then he looked at the real dragon's tooth beside it. What a fool he'd been to mistake one for the other.

The dragon suddenly became impatient again and began to pace up and down.

'HURRY UP THERE, BOY. I MAY NOT HAVE ANY TEETH BUT I SHALL SNAP YOUR THIN BRITTLE BONES WITH MY TONGUE IN A TRICE.'

Digory pulled off his last boot and the Horrible Gnasher Toast'em Firebreath opened his foul smelling jaws.

'Goodbye, sweet Enid!' Digory cried out and shut his eyes . . .

. . .BUT NOTHING HAPPENED.

Digory kept his eyes shut. He was so afraid that he wouldn't have opened them for a thousand groats. Still nothing happened. 'This torture is *even worse that being gobbled!*' he squirmed.

A Fate Worse than Death?

At last the Horrible Gnasher spoke.

'SWEET ENID, DID YOU SAY? IS SHE A MAIDEN? IS SHE REALLY SWEET?'

Digory couldn't believe his ears.

'She's a princess. She's my f-f-friend,' he blurted, opening one eye a crack.

'AH, SO SHE'S A PRINCESS INDEED! MMM, PRINCESSES ARE ALWAYS SWEET – EVEN THE HUFFY ONES.'

'She isn't huffy at all!' cried Digory.

'GOOD!' said the dragon. 'LET'S GO AND EAT HER ANYWAY. I HAVEN'T

HAD A JUICY PRINCESS FOR A MONTH.' And he turned tail and began to hurry down the passage towards the cave entrance. 'I'LL SPARE YOUR SCRAWNY BONES WHILE YOU LEAD ME TO HER CASTLE,' he called out hurriedly behind him. 'COME ALONG. ARE WE HEADING NORTH OR SOUTH, EH?'

To Be or Not to Be Gobbled

Digory didn't know what to do next. How could he lead Gnasher to Enid's castle? Yet if he refused he would certainly be eaten up and that would be the end of it. *At least I haven't been gobbled up so far, and the dragon himself is leading me out of this awful place*, he thought. *Maybe once we're in the woods I'll get a chance to escape.*

So he scrambled back into his armour, grabbed Burdock's sword and followed the

Horrible Gnasher down the passage towards fresh air and the forest.

Gnasher was waiting at the tunnel entrance.

'CLIMB UP THEN, QUICKLY,' he said. 'WHICH WAY TO BREAKFAST?'

Digory looked at the dragon's gnarled, scaly body silhouetted in the moonlight. His back was studded with horny spikes and from his shoulders sprouted leathery wings, the size of windmill sails.

'But I c-c-can't,' stuttered Digory.

'OH YES YOU CAN,' roared Gnasher and snorted a lick of flame at poor Digory's heels that made him jump like a firecracker and clamber up on the dragon's back.

Digory found a foothold on Gnasher's wing and heaved himself astride the dragon's shoulders. He clung to the cold, lizardy neck for all he was worth.

Slowly the dragon began to snake between the trees with Digory rolling on top until he found a clearing. Then, with a creak, Gnasher stretched out his huge wings and heaved them up high. As he brought them down again there was a deafening rush of air, and the dragon and his passenger lifted off the ground and rose sharply above the forest.

Digory's stomach sank to his boots. Gnasher lurched to the left and swooped to the right and Digory's stomach jumped into his throat. But as the dragon steadied his flight, Digory settled into the rhythm of the rocking motion and the roar of the wind through his helmet.

When he found the courage to open his eyes Digory was astonished at how beautiful the forest looked in the moonlight, from a dragon's-eye point of view. *One day I shall write a song about this*, he told himself. Then he remembered there was very little chance he would ever strum a lute again . . .

DIGORY THE NAVIGATOR

'WHICH WAY, THEN?' gasped the dragon

eagerly after they had circled the woods a few times to gain height.

Now, Digory had absolutely no idea which was the way to Enid's castle – he had lost King Widget's map a long time ago. But he *did* know that it was the last place he intended to lead a hungry dragon to. 'If we fly for long enough Gnasher will surely need to land and rest and then I'll have my chance to escape,' he thought to himself.

So he yelled, 'Carry on in this direction to the edge of the woods. Then follow the stream through the valley, cross a forest, over a hilltop, wind along the river and head towards the south.'

Gnasher seemed happy enough with these instructions so Digory shut his eyes once more to consider his situation.

Here I am, clinging to the back of a dragon who is expecting to gobble up the only friend I have in the world, and probably eat me afterwards, he thought. *And I don't know where I'm going, or what I shall do when I get there . . .*

He wondered what his mother, Betsy, would do if she were in his place. In his mind's eye he saw Betsy astride the dragon's back. With one hand she took a hammer from her apron pocket, hit the dragon hard upon the head, slaying it with one blow. Then as it fell from the sky, she whistled to an eagle passing overhead, leapt for its claws as it swooped low and then dropped on to a haystack below, somersaulting off and landing with a thud on her feet, with nothing but a corn stalk behind her ear to show for it.

Gnasher's roar brought him out of his daydream.

'AH! THAT MUST BE SWEET ENID.' And, sure enough, there in an orchard below was Enid out for an early morning walk.

Chapter Six

THE DRAGON MEETS HIS BREAKFAST

ONCE more Digory's dreadful sense of direction had brought him to the one place in the whole world that he didn't want to be! Thinking quickly he dropped his sword to try to warn his friend that she was in mortal danger. But it spun down crookedly and fell among some trees unnoticed.

'Enid, watch out!' he shouted with all his might. 'Run back to the castle and bolt the door.'

'FOOLISH BOY!' growled the Horrible Gnasher, and he dropped down, swooping in a low circle, and landed at Enid's feet, tipping Digory off his back and into a muddy ditch.

Digory heaved himself out and clambered to Enid's side. She was frozen to the spot. Her hands trembled but her eyes were fiery.

'We're not afraid of d-dragon's here,' she said bravely. 'Do you know who this knight is?'

Gnasher's stomach rumbled like echoing thunder.

'YES, YES,' he growled impatiently. 'I KNOW WHO HE IS AND I KNOW WHO HE ISN'T AND I'M IN NO MOOD FOR POLITE CONVERSATION. JUST RE-MOVE THAT JEWELLERY, IF YOU PLEASE – I AM VERY, VERY HUNGRY!'

Enid stood straight and tall and shook her hodgepig hair defiantly.

'No, I will not,' she said, stamping her foot like a huffy princess.

Digory watched Enid's bravery shine out of her like the rays of the sun. He knew at once what he must do. Hoping to give his friend a chance of escape Sir Digory the True Knight stood forward.

'Eat me first, dragon,' he insisted. 'I know you intend to gobble us both and the princess will taste much sweeter after me.' It was the only way left to save her.

'Oh Digory, no!' cried Enid desperately. But the Horrible Gnasher Toast'em Firebreath had heard enough. Never had he come across such a fuss and bother over a spot of break-fast. With a grunt of irritation he opened his jaws and swallowed Digory in one mouthful. And then, before she had time to faint, he ate Enid too.

Chapter Seven

DIGORY FINDS HIMSELF
IN A SLIMY, DARK PLACE

DIGORY slid down the dragon's throat and found himself in a slimy, dark, foul smelling place, ankle deep in warm slops that bubbled and hissed. Before he had time to work out what had happened something knocked him over and fell on top of him in the slime.

'Help!' screamed Enid.

'Gbblluuurbulleugh!' spluttered Digory. The two friends tried to sit up in the stinking slosh and immediately realised what had happened.

'We must be dead!' exclaimed Digory.

'No, we're alive!' laughed Enid.

Then they both paused. . .

'WE'RE IN A DRAGON'S STOMACH!!' they shrieked and clutched each other in the dark.

However, before you could say 'digestive juices' Digory and Enid were deafened by a belly-shaking roar. The Horrible Gnasher Toast'em Firebreath coughed his breakfast out on to the grass and with a loud bang turned into a horse's nosebag!

Chapter Eight

WHAT??!

WHEN Digory and Enid had checked that all their arms and legs were ungobbled they looked around for the dragon. But all they could see, lying before them in a patch of nettles, was a large nosebag stuffed with fresh hay and, to their astonishment, Barley the carthorse shuffling suspiciously round it.

Under a tree nearby, Digory spotted Burdock's sword.

'What happened?' asked Enid weakly.

What happened indeed? Digory and Enid were to ask themselves that question a thousand times in their long, happy lives. But unfortunately the only creature who knew the answer was Barley – and she never heard the question. And even if she *had* heard the question Barley could never have told them that she'd been ambling through the orchard, taking the very-long-and-hungry-route back to Batty-by-Noodle, daydreaming of nose-bags of delicious hay, when a sword had fallen out of the sky and landed on her head.

As she recovered, and stumbled back to her feet, she was amazed to see an enormous

dragon eat her master right there before her eyes. Picking up the sword in her teeth Barley had charged valiantly at the Horrible Gnasher Toast'em Firebreath – too late to stop him swallowing the Princess as well but sudden enough to catch him off guard and strike him in the tail – whereupon there was a loud bang and the dragon coughed up Digory and Enid and turned into a nosebag of the sweetest smelling hay Barley had ever dreamed of.

Well, that is exactly what happened indeed, but Barley could never tell the tale, and as it was not an easy story to guess no one ever learnt the truth.

Digory and Enid were completely bamboozled by their escape and the disappearance of the Horrible Gnasher. But they didn't spend any time looking for him. They were just content to be reunited and unchewed.

'You were the bravest Knight in the Kingdom,' beamed Enid.

'No, you were the bravest,' insisted Digory.

'No, *you* were the bravest . . .'

'No, *you* were the bravest . . .'

And so they argued happily all the way back to King Widget's castle.

Chapter Nine

THE KING REMEMBERS

DIGORY and Enid found King Widget hunting for something under the benches in the banqueting hall. The King was very pleased to see Digory again, although he'd quite forgotten why he'd sent him off in the first place.

'Welcome back, Diggers!' he said, hugging

him like a son. 'Been on your holidays, eh? Do anything interesting?'

Digory smiled to himself.

'I certainly wasn't bored, Your Highness,' he said.

Enid reached up to whisper in her father's ear.

'Oddsbodikins! In a dragon's belly, eh?' the King exclaimed. 'Seems a funny place to spend your holidays if you don't mind me saying, lad,' he chuckled. 'You young knights are full of imagination. Anyway, glad you're back. I've got a little . . . you know . . . do this, do that sort of thing . . .' and he pulled a long list of 'Jobs to do on Friday' from an inside pocket of his cloak. 'Shouldn't take you long, eh. Now, has anyone seen my purple doo-dahs, or are they green . . . um . . . one goes up and one goes down . . .' and he shuffled off scratching his head.

Digory looked at the list happily. Anything to be done at the castle *would* be a holiday after his last adventure.

As he glanced through the jobs his eye caught the last one which read:

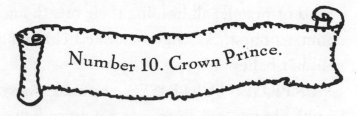

Number 10. Crown Prince.

It seemed that although the King could not remember the colour of his doo-dahs he had not forgotten his wish to make Digory a prince.

DIGORY A PRINCE

And so, when all the jobs were done that Friday, Sir Digory cleaned himself up, polished his tin boots and went to knock shyly on the door of the throne room. Enid opened the door and, to his surprise, gave him a big wink. Then she stepped aside. Behind her stood the King and Queen, smiling, in their best cloaks and crowns, and behind them the great chamber was packed with a jostling crowd of people, all holding their breath and about to burst. As Digory looked closer he couldn't believe his eyes . . .

'SURPRISE, SURPRISE!' shouted Betsy, scrubbed pink and clean as a newborn babe.

'BRAVO!' cried his father, sat up on the shoulders of Arthur, Tom and Ethelburg.

'THREE CHEERS FOR THE PRINCE!' boomed King Paunch. 'HIP, HIP, HOORAY!' And all the villagers of Batty-by-Noodle clapped and whooped and whistled.

Sure enough, they had travelled, every one, by horse, cart and farm wagon to celebrate the crowning of young Digory the Dragon Slayer, and none of them was prouder than Betsy the blacksmith.

'Ooh, I've come over all rusty red,' she beamed as she burst forward and hugged him tight. And Digory was so pleased to see her that a tear rolled down his cheek and sizzled on hers.

Time for a Happy Ending?

And so it was that an ordinary sort of boy with lanky legs, ginger hair and a nose like a chipolata turned out to be not so ordinary after all. He became Prince Digory of Widget Castle. But best of all he became a true knight and he found a true friend.

On Saturdays Digory did useful things for the King and on Sunday afternoons Enid pretended to be a Princess in Peril and Digory saved her.

One day, while fooling around, Digory discovered that if he made a wish and then dropped Burdock's sword the wish would come true – as if the magic took a bit of a nudge to warm up.

'Magic sword, eh?' muttered King Widget admiringly. 'Jolly useful sort of thing for . . . um . . . for a . . . you know . . . a what-next-and-all-of-a-sudden!'

Digory didn't know. With a sigh he took a guess. 'Is it a game, Your Majesty?'

'No, no, no!' chuckled the King. He picked up the hem of his cloak and began to gallop around the courtyard on an imaginary charger, waving the sword wildly in the air. 'You know, Diggers . . .' he cried, '. . . danger and daring . . . with lots of, um, danger . . .'

'You mean an adventure, Your Majesty?' suggested Digory.

'Exactly!' cried the King. 'Usual sort of thing for a Prince. Sure to come up now and then. Won't be any trouble for a boy like you.'

'Oh dear!' groaned Digory. 'I thought I was having a happy ending.'

But I don't think it was quite time for that yet, do you?

A NOTE ON THE AUTHOR

Angela McAllister is the author of over fifty books for children, several of which she has illustrated herself. Angela has two children who are fantastic bookworms and a brilliant inspiration. She lives with her family in a crumbly 16th Century cottage with an unruly garden on the edge of Cranborne Chase. This is Angela's sixth book for Bloomsbury.

A NOTE ON THE ILLUSTRATOR

Ian Beck is the author and illustrator of several books for children. He is well known for illustrating many wonderful and familiar nursery rhymes as well as winning gold with three of his books in the Right Start Best Toy Awards. He lives in London with his wife and children. This is Ian's first book for Bloomsbury.